ALL THE WAY TO
LHASA

A TALE FROM TIBET

Retelling & Art by

BARBARA HELEN BERGER

Philomel Books • New York

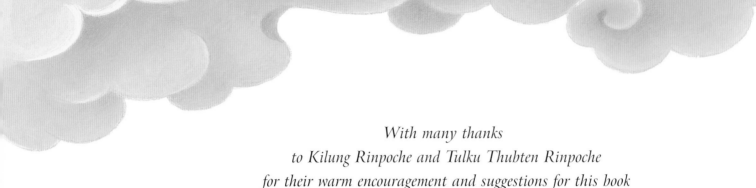

*With many thanks
to Kilung Rinpoche and Tulku Thubten Rinpoche
for their warm encouragement and suggestions for this book*

———————————————

Patricia Lee Gauch, Editor

Copyright © 2002 by Barbara Helen Berger. All rights reserved.
This book, or parts thereof, may not be reproduced in any form without permission in writing
from the publisher, Philomel Books, a division of Penguin Putnam Books for Young Readers,
345 Hudson Street, New York, NY 10014. Philomel Books, Reg. U.S. Pat. & Tm. Off.
Published simultaneously in Canada. Printed in Hong Kong by South China Printing Co. (1988) Ltd.

Book design by Gunta Alexander. The text is set in Arrus Bold.
The art was done in acrylic, colored pencil, and gouache on hot pressed watercolor paper.

Library of Congress Cataloging-in-Publication Data
Berger, Barbara Helen, 1945 Mar. 1–   All the way to Lhasa : a tale from Tibet /
retelling & art by Barbara Helen Berger.
p. cm. Based on a story told to the author by Lama Tharchin Rinpoche.
Summary: A boy and his yak persevere along the difficult way to the holy city of Lhasa and
succeed where others fail. [1. Folklore—China—Tibet.] I. Title. PZ8.1.B4163 Al 2002
398.2'09515—dc21 [E] 2001054560   ISBN 0-399-23387-3
1 3 5 7 9 10 8 6 4 2
First Impression

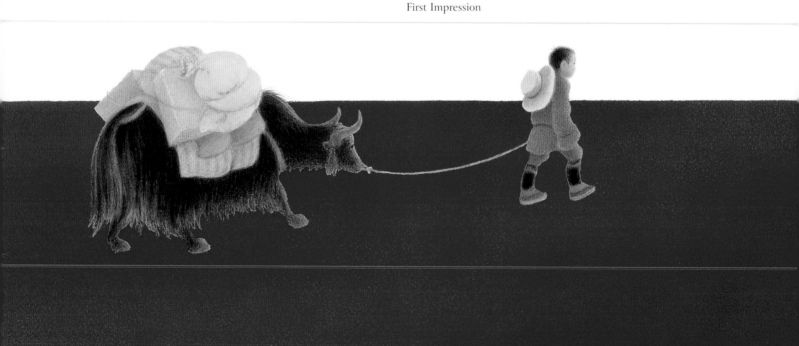

I heard this story told by Lama Tharchin Rinpoche,
who was born in Tibet. With his kind permission,
I have freely adapted it from the oral source to a picture book,
trying to keep the essence.
I offer this retelling in deepest gratitude
to Lama Tharchin Rinpoche,
my inspiring teacher.

Long ago in the land of Tibet,

an old woman sat by the road
to the holy city of Lhasa.

A horse and rider came galloping up to her.

"How far is it to Lhasa?"

"Very far," said the old woman,

"you'll never make it there before night."
But the rider kicked his horse
and galloped off as fast as a horse can run.

Then a boy came walking along with his yak,
one foot in front of the other.
"How far is it to Lhasa?"
"Very far," said the old woman,

"but you can make it there before night."
So the boy gave his yak a gentle tug
and kept on walking.

One foot in front of the other,

he climbed a steep and windy slope.

He thought the torrents would sweep him away.

He thought he would be lost in the snows.

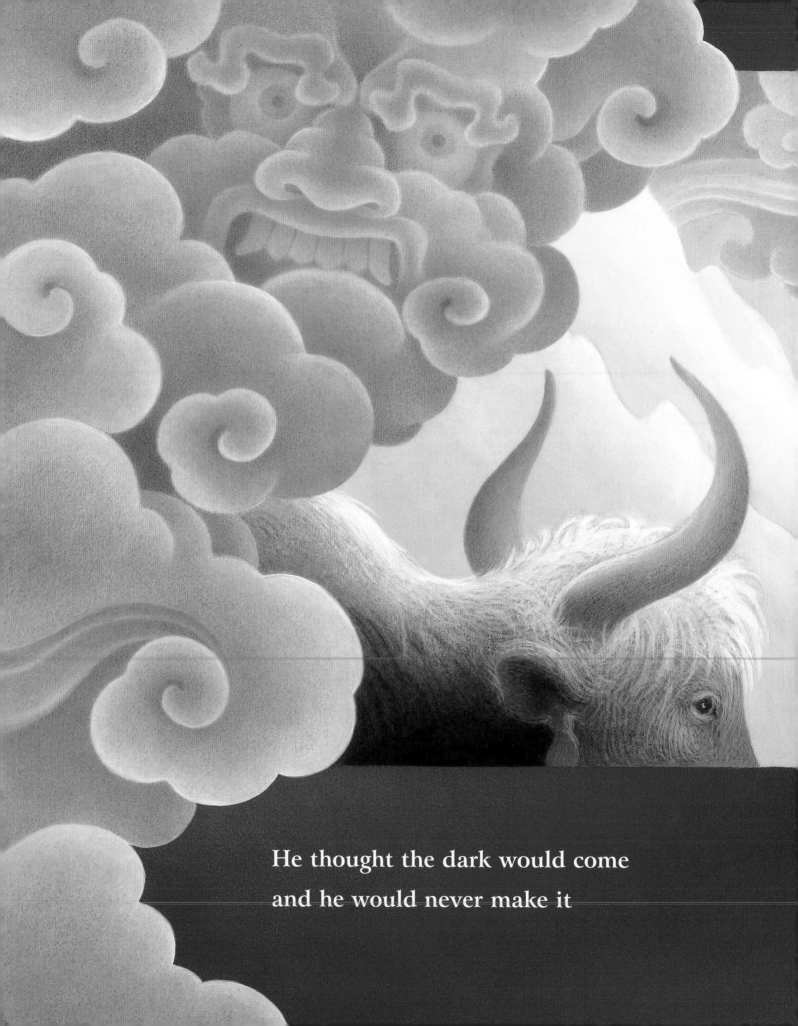

He thought the dark would come
and he would never make it

to the holy city of Lhasa.

But still the boy kept walking,
on and on with his steady yak,

one foot in front of the other.

Then he came to a fallen horse and rider.

They had run so hard, they could run no more.

And there they lay, snoring.

The boy wanted to lie down too.
But he gave his yak a gentle tug
and kept on walking.

Then, in the last rays of sun before night,

he heard deep horns calling.

He heard bells, *si li li*,
and drums, *dro lo lo*.

Emaho! He had made it—

one foot in front of the other,

all the way

to the holy city of Lhasa.

A Note from the Author

Hidden by the high Himalaya Mountains, Lhasa was hardly known to the rest of the world for centuries. But to the Tibetan people it has always been a sacred place. It is the capital city, home of a great temple, and the goal of many journeys.

To go there, Tibetans have crossed the valleys, plains and snowy passes of their country, the highest land on earth. Like the boy in the tale, they have gone on foot. They have gone with horses. They have gone with yaks bearing the heavy loads. In wind and snow, a coat lined with the wooly hair of a yak will keep a traveler warm.

Along the way, there are prayers carved into the stones. *Om mani padme hum* is everywhere. This is the favorite mantra of Tibet, shown in the tale as the boy walks by. Chanted, murmured and sung like a flowing stream, it is a prayer of great compassion for all beings. Tibetans feel it is a blessing even to hear or see the syllables.

Flags are printed with prayers and strung up in high places. They flutter and snap in the wind, blessing all who pass. And there are white stupas, or shrines. These can help a traveler remember the nature of his journey. With its dome and golden spire, every stupa represents the mind of enlightenment. One of them is an ancient gate to Lhasa. The boy walks through it to enter the city at last.

In this simple tale, Lhasa can stand as a symbol to anyone, anywhere. We all have our own highest hope, and our own journey. May we keep going like the boy and his yak. May all of us reach our own shining goal. And may peace and happiness spread—like a sun rising over the mountains—to all beings.